Praise for *Glass Labyrinth*

"Spencer's work is an ethereal meditation on loneliness, grief, and the relentless swirl of life. The 'choose a pathway' format adds nuance to the dreamy feel of the prose. Phrases landed within my consciousness and left ripples."

—Beth Cato, two-time Rhysling Award winner and author of *A Thousand Recipes for Revenge*

"*Glass Labyrinth* is brilliant. Absolutely brilliant. Not only the format, but also the poetry it contains. I recognized myself in these verses, and my characters, and also a twin sister who never actually existed. It is evocative, magical, and beautiful but wholly accessible even to people who are brand new to reading poetry. It is a book that I will definitely get lost (and rediscovered) in again and again."

—Rhonda Parrish, author and anthology editor

"In this, her phenomenal third collection of poems, Spencer's indelible voice serves as a guide on a journey that invites us readers along the way to excavate the intricacies of memory. She weaves her verse with seductive, stringent image and flavor; each reading yields discoveries, unveiling the unconscious modes by which we access our creative capacity for healing."

—Sonya Wohletz, author of *One Row After/ Bir Sıra Sonra*

"To read *Glass Labyrinth* is to enter the surreal world of dreams and memory. Its warp and weft might not serve as a carpet except perhaps, of the flying sort, but would serve well as fiber art for your dysfunctional family room. Falling into this rabbit hole reveals a world of fireflies, ants, snails, and bathing in a bathtub full of dandelions. At the bottom is the landing place of rocks and soil and rot where tomatoes and orchids grow fitfully while lightning bugs flash on and off. It also contains perhaps the best definition of a poem ever written. It's a fun romp to read it straight through. I urge you to take every alternate path to experience the richness of this adventure tale disguised as a book of poetry"

—Emily Moon, author of *It's Just You and Me, Miss Moon*

"This collection surprised me in the best way. It explores identity, memory, personal growth, and the way we hold on to things we can't quite explain, unanswered questions, versions of ourselves, feelings we haven't figured out how to let go of."

—Kaitlyn Marquart, author of *Amber Luna: My Bright Light*

"*Glass Labyrinth* embodies the nuanced and questioning life of its writer. Each poem is something enticingly new, each page another adventure into a world of hopes and dreams. Spencer explores experience and possibility with every word, turning a life of chaotic multitudes into a quaint and curious collection. Her poetry reflects powerful simplicities as though they were moonlight on water —a fun and unforgettable read."

—Caidan Walker, Editor-in-Chief of *Lucky Lizard Journal*

"Spencer's book encapsulates the mess of decision making when you don't know exactly where life will lead you. Reading these poems felt like living a whole lifetime, and somehow, I came out the other side feeling a little more healed than when I began."

—Sarah, Founder of *Sad Girl Diaries*—An Online Literary Magazine

Glass Labyrinth

poems

Hailey Spencer

Thirty West
Publishing

10 YEARS
2015-2025

Glass Labyrinth

ISBN-13: 979-8-9895422-8-4

Cover design and artwork by Carolyn Brandt

Edited by Olivia Zarzycki and Josh Dale

Author photo by Amy Deyerle-Smith

Printed in the U.S.A.

For more titles and inquiries, please visit:

www.thirtywestph.com

*This book is dedicated to all
the strangest years of my life*

*and to all the people who
helped me through them.*

Table of Contents

Glass Labyrinth

Introduction

she can't stop thinking about her childhood backyard, a quarter-acre with fireflies in the crabapple tree. she can't stop thinking about the summer of boxelder bugs, how they tore through the yard and burrowed their way into the carpet. she remembers sunshine, not these gray northwestern skies. she is an adult now, well-acquainted with the rain and hills. she maps out the child she used to be and the woman she is becoming, and she almost understands.

a poem is such a loose, uncanny thing, like her own heart and the way she wants to vivisect it. a poem is a quagmire, an algebraic formula and she can't make her way from beginning to end. a poem is a gaping wound. she is almost thirty years old. she is still only five years old. the years spin out of order like a film reel spliced together by a child.

this year asks questions. twenty-dollar gift cards for completing job interviews. dissociation while finally watching Carrie. that night at the open mic when the theme was "it will be all right" and she couldn't find a single poem to read. this is no longer the ease of early 20s, the everything-that's-done-can-be-undoneness. she spends more time on what-ifs and less time writing, then more time writing and then less again. this year, she baptizes herself under a sky that won't let up, dark morning under amber crush of leaves and a shadow that won't stay glued against her feet.

in a bathtub full of salt, she asks a question to the notepad perched upon her knee. she keeps asking until the water goes cold and she's forced back into bed, blanket pulled up over her head to keep her safe through winter.

and there are choices, and things that do not feel like choices but still are, and she doesn't know how to make them. she is frozen in the face of the job she left, the year everyone started going out again and the things that happened next. there is a backyard surrounded by bamboo and a single tomato that's split open on the vine. things left alone too long begin to wander, epiphytic roots that climb out of their soil, and maybe this year, she is more metaphor than girl.

so when every question leads into another

she prays she'll find a way to answer them.

Situation #1

You are:

Lying in a bath of dried dandelion heads, contemplating the
death of summer and the heavy bags of soil you have left
propped against the tub. Your head leans back against the
bathtub's slant, imagining a window through which you can see
the moon.

And you:

a)   Climb out of the tub, holding on to the edges as you
      peel skin from ceramic, yellow petals clinging to your
      hips.

b)   Stay submerged. Let the gentle music play across your
      sternum. Look left toward the open doorway, look
      right toward the pink and yellow wall. Breathe deeply
      as the flowers grow damp and gray.

c)   Heap the dandelions out of the tub and into a pile in
      your yard, which you will burn into the night, wildfire
      season non-withstanding. Let the smoke coat the
      inner corridors of your lungs.

If a, go to page 17.
If b, go to page 18.
If c, go to page 19.

Obtainment

You peel the petals off of your hips and collect them in a bag. The carnage of the stems is left to clog your rusty drains. You inhabit this strange skin, as much as you meant to exit it.

You have obtained a bag of petals.

If you bury it in a box carved from pine, go to page 20.
*If you weave a hempen string through it and
wear it around your neck, go to page 21.*

Decay

You lie alone beneath the gray and wait.

Over time, flowers rot and expand until they cover you all the way up to your neck, above your neck, above your head as they wrap around your windpipe. Gray sludge surrounds you. This is no way to survive the winter. This is a tomb, although it need not be.

You:

a)   Climb out. This is not your tomb, not your destiny to die prematurely, and your breath is stronger than dead flowers ever were. You cough, and yellow sap trickles from your lips.

b)   Remain submerged.

If a, go to page 17.
If b, go to page 23.

Consecration

A packet of matches, struck once in the dandelion pile in your backyard, unravels itself into flame at once. Smoke cascades into the mountains, fills the salmon habitats with ash. Your cabin's attic smells like campfire smoke for weeks.

With soot attaching itself to balcony doors, the city people stay inside. Night janitors attend to empty buildings, gas masks hanging over half-closed lips.

Standing close to the smoke and breathing in, you acknowledge that for the rest of your life, you will hold scars shaped like dandelions in your lungs. After all of this, to stay alive means something must come next.

Do you:

    a)   Flee the city and seek out another home?

    b)   Stay, and build your garden in the ashes?

    c)   Stay, and lie down in the river with the coughing fish?

If a, go to page 24.
If b, go to page 22.
If c, go to page 18.

Burial

In the back of your childhood closet is a trap door,
underneath which, a foundation full of fiberglass and ants,
underneath which, only earth.

You dig your nails into soft soil, embedding bits
of exoskeleton and other things you'd prefer not to think about
against the lowers layers of your skin—

finally, a box of pine, rotten hinges, pristine wood.

Fill it with the heads of dandelions and
a notecard filled with scribbles which describe
the last thing you imagined when you played here
as a child.

You are no longer a child.

Do you:

a)   Leave it buried?

b)   Dig it up, and count the petals one by one?

If a, you no longer have the petals. Go to page 26.
If b, go to page 27.

Albatross

And if every poem is a whisper around the throat
forgive yourself.
And if this thing around your neck reshapes your spine,
forgive yourself.

There is only so much one small neck can carry,
be it bird, or stone, or crushed yellow petals.

There is only so much one person can forgive.

Do you:

    a)   forgive yourself?

If a, go to page 22.

Horticulture

*Sieve rocks out of the soil and fill a jar. Feed life into the
ground with slick red leaves. Wait for a thousand nights*

and then one more.

The moon is full, and you remember the child you once were,
the necklaces with chunky beads you wore even when digging
in your yard. You remember what it was you wanted to tell her,
that girl in the overalls with a smile over half her face, the girl
who doesn't need forgiveness after all, only to be seen and
understood.

Wait until moonrise, when your tongue is at its loosest and
your throat is clear. Under the lamplight of the sky, the wind
whispers a series of questions. Repeat them back until you
forget your own name, until you forget

how lonely it is here in the empty city

(but you never will forget that little girl).

Go to page 28.

Renewal

What they won't tell you about being buried in a sludge of flowers:

a) It is vast, infinite, a world unto itself.

b) You deserve to hurt like this. You have done harm in this world, and to die surrounded by something which was once beautiful and has now gone to rot is the only suitable ending for a creature such as you.

c) It is boring.

If a, go to page 26.
If b, go to page 21.
If c, go to page 25.

Stasis

for years, you lie alone on a hard mattress and have the same dream every single night. in a forest that is also a city and does not exist, there sits a house covered in honeysuckle and ivy, a gorgeous mess of vines. the house is a part of the forest, snails creeping along the siding. there is a spider in the corner that does not wish you ill and eats the ants that trickle in the cracks. you are only as alone as you wish to be.

under gray skies, you wake up from the dream and go to work.

the forever house, not just place but destination. you will have a job, a place to rest, a fireplace through the winter. the bills never too high, the bathtub never leaking. these days you no longer believe in the old man in the sky who grants wishes, can only accept a different sort of god, but still, you pray for it as tears remain trapped in your eyes. *oh lord, grant me stagnation, grant me freedom from the obscenity of change, do not let me do a thing that cannot be undone.*

think of your childhood, the places you lived and how any amount of time felt like forever, about the earthquakes and the fissures they created, how *safe* could mean so many different things and sometimes not a goddamn thing at all. the forever house, the place you lived before the bad things happened, the place you will return to when the bad things end.

Go to page 28.

Mundanity

So it's boring.

So you walk through the November yellow-gray, rotten petals soldered to your skin, and it bores into you like the dream in which you walk down the same hallway over and over, rows of doors and nothing behind any one of them.

So you carry yourself like a bucket of gray water, heavy and sloshing over the edges.

So most mornings as you make breakfast, you look at the blue bowl, floral pattern around the edges, that cost $25 to replace after the previous one broke in the microwave, and imagine it smashing to the floor, shards of ceramic that you won't manage to clean up all the way, that will lodge their way into the skin between your toes.

So the sun against your skin feels no different than the cold night air.

So there are ghosts living between the vertebrae of your spine, and you are tired of always living in the past.

So there's this thing you don't understand inside your ribs. You name it motion sickness, name it a broken rearview mirror, name it love without forgiveness, name it nothing and admit that all you know is there's an emergency inside your bones that can't be fixed by wishful thinking.

So you hear the whispered words "forever house," and you imagine yourself reaching it, bones ground down and ceramic between your toes, and maybe you can rest, and is this the point of everything, just rest?

So you wonder, could there possibly be more, and every doorway leads only to the past, and maybe this is your answer if you can bear to look.

Go to page 28.

Considerations

millimeter yellow petals // bathwater sluiced from dandelion sap // afterbirth // crescent moon at dusk // loving the world you were born into // afterdeath // dandelion wine at the liquor store // accidents of fate // accidents of: no such thing as fate // ants digging tunnels in the place where you buried the petals // your own body, buried under the petals // ends at last // aftermath // hating the world because you were born into it // the last time that you see someone you love // love lapsed // psychological mishaps // fluffy white strands // regeneration // roots grafted to porcelain // farmer's almanac, predicting rain at last // rain that lasts for days until the roads erode and rivers fill with sand // sandbags split at seams // spiderweb dreams // the last time you see someone you never want to see again

Go to page 28.

Perseverate

one to two hundred petals *(you keep having to start over)* on a
dandelion, and
            who loves who this time again?
                        and you, so tired
from all of the digging *(maybe somewhere around one
hundred fifty)*
            of things that aren't your grave
where will you sit when it's over?

       is there a sharp pain behind your left eye, or *(one
hundred seventy-two—no, three)*
            just the ache of something left behind?

and are you exhausted yet *(two hundred twelve)*
and will you be forgiven?

Go to page 28.

first-grade class assignment

start with childhood. seven years old and asked to write a story for the first time. requirements: must contain a problem and solution. eager to get started, she fills three pieces of final draft paper in her carefulest scrawl.

Problem:
a frog needs glasses but has no money

Solution:
he opens up a lemonade stand

Problem
when she was two, her sister almost died and kept almost dying, and her mother was in the hospital for weeks

Solution:
to stay with worried grandparents, to refuse to nap in case something might happen while she slept

Problem:
how to talk about the things that've happened, and the ways they've changed her, without casting blame on anyone

Solution:
she buries it deep inside her chest, lets it grow alongside her own heartbeat, tells it over and over like a story 'til it doesn't hurt

Problem:
*her chest is full of soil
and the things she's planted turn out to be seeds.*

Continue to page 29.

Situation #2

You are:

Crouched along a riverbed, sieving ashes from the water and collecting them in an envelope. The gray eats into your cuticles, like you are wearing fingers of the dead. The mud between your toenails has gone cold.

And you:

a) Think again about the forever house. Imagine a world of fireflies landing on your shoulders after the summer festival, the strawberries that you will gorge upon. Visualize it so clearly that a path emerges in the space before your eyes, then follow it.

b) Let the wound speak first, despite its brittle thorns.

c) Forget the house, forget the wound, think only of what is in front of you and go toward it. Cross the river. Walk until you reach a hill, then begin your ascent. Let sweat pool in the dip beneath your spine.

If a, go to page 30.
If b, go to page 38.
If c, go to page 42.

In the Forever Yard

bright moss grows from the tops of concrete cinder blocks even when the sun does not shine down. Your feet grow soft, uncalloused. You learn to identify each type of moth and leave a lantern out in the night so they have somewhere to fly home to.

In the forever yard, you eat watermelon from the vine and let the juices trickle down your arms, sticky-sweet, easily rinsed off. The seeds slip from your lips back to the soil, preparing for the summer, which comes often and exactly when you need it.

In the forever yard, lightning bugs land on your skin and stay there even through the storms.

And as you prayed for, nothing ever changes.

You are safe.

If you stay at the forever house, go to page 31.
If you leave, go to page 32.

(un)desiccate

The
    vines

creep
their way around

the walls
    you dip their
     roots in

       salt   water
   they grow

   in spite
     of
    your tender
      care

The vines consume the structure brick by brick.

If you move on, go to page 36.
If you lie down in the ruins and weep, go to page 37.

Haunting

The forever house becomes grown over with ivy, moss, and one day the spindly roots of trees, although you will not live to see that part. The bamboo that once maintained your privacy is torn down by the same morning glory you pulled out one summer, laying salt on the roots so it would not return. It was supposed to be easy, so you ignored the things that didn't go as planned, even when the bathtub pulled away from the floor and left water in the walls, just as they promised it wouldn't.

One day, sunlight will glitter off of broken windows, preparing for the ants to return home.

But long before this can occur, you return to the forever house for one last visit. Someone else lives there now, a family with children, and your chest feels hollow at the image of the swing-set they've put in, smooth wood and nails. You feel yourself a ghost laid over someone else's life.

Do you:

a) Knock on the door and wait to be let in.

b) Walk on and leave the past where it belongs.

c) [Choose only if you have a bag of petals] Leave a trail of dandelions to mark your pathway home.

If a, go to page 33.
If b, go to page 38.
If c, go to 34.

Vigil

You wait
on the creaking porch step
          for a day
                         and a night
until it's clear that no one's coming
and you can't get warm.

You shiver and shake, imagine warm
                    earth,
                                        warmer
               pine.

you set
the forever house on fire,
and this
                    is no way to end a story.

When you awake in a pile of ashes,

don't forgive yourself.

Rub your
fingers over
          cheekbone and tell me what it means
to die of frostbite.

Show me how
to steep my bones into a broth
and maybe then we'll both get through the winter.

When springtime comes, sit very quiet   and still.
Maybe then you'll hear the birds

and maybe they'll forgive you.

If you hear the chatter of insects, go to page 34.
If you hear only the pounding of questions,
go to page 39.

Entomology

Trails of petals may attract insects of the following classifications:

Ant: omen of past deaths. leftover bits, taken away on the back of something strong.

Butterfly: symbol of beauty and growth, migration over multiple generations.

Caterpillar: larval state of Lepidoptera order, which dissolve into goo as they transform.

Cicada: screams at night from fear, from lack of answers. rhythm in a chaotic universe.

Fruit Fly: lazy circles around compost heap. sweetness of things gone to rot.

Honey Bee: social, necessary to human survival.

Ladybug: art of escape. crawling despite access to wings.

Locust: grasshoppers, under correct conditions to change color, swarm, and destroy.

Maggot: larval stage of flies. associated with decay. surgical removal of dying parts; renewal.

Moth: many sub-species lack a mouth, only consuming nutrients in their larval stage. *(See: Caterpillar)*

Nymph: larval stage of grasshoppers. undergoes five phases of molting before adulthood.

Praying Mantis: named for posture which mimics human prayer.

Silk Worm: larval state of the silk moth. domesticated for textiles and no longer live in the wild.

Termite: ability to deconstruct something so thoroughly that it will collapse from inside out.

Wasp: at end of life, they lay their eggs in figs and are digested by the fruit.

Go to page 47.

reintegration

wake up cocooned and wholly unafraid
wrapped up inside your lover's careful arms.
they promised you that life would not be hard.
nothing bad can touch you here.
yellow light through open window.

there is nothing eating at your stomach, no strange acid
clawing at your throat. nothing bad will happen to you today,
or any day.
life is easy, they promised.

(and if this lack of history unsettles you, remember this:

that where there is poison, there is also a seed
so when you swallow poison, wash it down
with funeral dirt
and tears.

it will not grow for a long time. it may be that it does not grow
at all. it may be that it sprouts inside your lungs and its roots
graft themselves to your ribs and your spine

and only you will see
what has grown there.)

Go to page 47.

after the house comes down

you will cry every day for a year

reading of the devastation in the newspaper
        and in petals and mushrooms that line
        the bottom of your teacup.

there are three ways to make the crying stop:
        the pulse of air from trees until your sobbing is absorbed;
        a hole you dug yourself, unsprouted seeds still in the soil;
        a mirror full of faces in which none looks like your own.

and there are those who will tell you not to cry over a house
no matter how tattooed it was upon your bones
or what you find in the ground as you dig up your garden

and pray last summer's garlic finally sprouts.

Go to page 47.

Trauma Work

At the therapist's office, you are given a list of questions to complete.

1. *Where do you feel it in your body?*
2. *What is the youngest you remember feeling these sensations?*
3. *Who else was there, and what did they do?*
4. *Are you ready to face it?*
5. *Are you ready to keep facing it?*
6. *Can you face it if it never heals?*

*If you answer every question with a question,
go to page 39.*
*If you answer every question with a lie,
go to page 40.*

other lines of inquiry

1. *I feel it in the calcified spaces between my ankles and my ribs, underneath the porcelain of my cheeks. Can you tell me what lightning it is that lives beneath my skin? Can you tell me how to keep myself from burning?*

2. *When I was five I got lost in the grocery store and every mother was wearing the same floral leggings, and icicles started running down my cheeks, and my own mom finally found me in the condom aisle. Can you tell me why this happened?*

3. *Who else should have been there?*

4. *What happens if I'm not ready?*

5. *In fifth grade, we were told that with careful footing, you can stand on all the eggs in a carton without breaking a single one, that when standing upright they're so much less fragile than you'd think. Is it true? Can you prove it to me, please?*

6. *Can I survive without at least trying to face it?*

Go to page 47.

out-of-body

1. *I don't.*
2. *I didn't.*
3. *No one.*
4. *Of course.*
5. *Of course.*
6. *Of course.*

"Then face it."

You can't.

If you agree to return next week, go to page 41.
If you leave and never come back, go to page 46.

Self-Help

Step 1: Mindfulness. Observe the world around you. ~~Wonder why you don't feel better.~~ Notice the sunflowers growing higher than your head. ~~Wonder why you are a person and not a sunflower.~~ Listen to the neighbors' feet upstairs. ~~Wonder if they are happy.~~

Step 2: Listen to your body. Lay on the floor and count your heartbeats. ~~Wonder why it's all so hard to bear.~~ Breathe out for more counts than you breathe in for. Let the sadness visit. Dust the corners and clear the shelves so it has plenty of room. ~~Wonder what is the point, when there is so much sad to carry with you.~~ Give yourself room to cry. Go slow if you need to. ~~Wonder how you are expected to hold down a job now that you're moving slow and giving space to all these feelings.~~

Step 3: Radical acceptance. See the situation you are in and not the one you wish you were in. This is called experiencing life. This is called living in the world and not just in your head. ~~Wonder what was so wrong, really, with the life you had been living in your head.~~

Step 4: Process your feelings by embodying them. You are not just a mind, though you often tell yourself you are. This is why you do things that you do not understand. The body is a player, not a scoreboard. ~~Wonder why nobody told you this before now.~~ There are leaves rotting on the ground outside. Take a moment to notice how they feel beneath your feet.

Go to page 47.

the boulder

There is a field of sunflowers at the top of the hill and you
run toward it but you can't reach it, you run toward
it but you can't reach it, there is a wooden sign
three-quarters of the way up the hill that reads

ARE YOU FUCKING UP THIS WORK?

a)   You will not fuck up this work. There is only a quarter
of a hill left before you can rest in a field of sunflowers
and dreams.

b)   The question trips you up and tears you open. You go
down the hill on heavy feet, enter your home, and
close and lock the door.

If a, go to page 43.
If b, go to page 45.

bo ld

at the top   you

run   toward

a wooden sign

that reads

ARE YOU

a)   You have to keep going.

b)   It's no one's business what you're fucking up.

If a, go to page 44.
If b, go to page 46.

you

run

to

a)   There is no top of the hill

b)   is there?

Go to page 47.

halfway-dinner

Lay the table for the wintertime, then
leave and do not return to taste from it. People
are always apt to do such useless things;

preparing a bomb shelter for a crisis that never comes.

There is no soup for your winter table,
only animal fat, the skin of the gopher
found beneath the front porch.

Those who want real sustenance must tend to it themselves
and none of us have been our best this year.

Salt the fat heavily.

Salt until there are no pillars left, then
set the table, lay the serving bowl
beneath the crack in the ceiling

where rainwater filters in.

Go to page 47.

disintegration

ahuva[1] said "I will not fuck up this work"
and you admire her confidence.
think, pillars of salt,

think, if you could just keep your fucking eyes shut,
the underworld would have no reason to swallow
any part of you.

and what work is it, and
how badly do you think you'll fuck it up?

think, crying on the floor, carpet
burns against your ankles,
think of all the deaths and lives
you've already been through.

think,
I can do this, but not forever,
and take a moment to feel it in your body,
and do not try to leave your body,

no matter how you ache to run away.
let pillars of salt run down your cheeks,
and if you must look back

forgive yourself.

Go to page 47.

---

[1] ahuva s. zavlasky is the author of *Between These Borders Wanders a Golem,* a
hybrid text which includes the piece "I WILL NOT FUCK UP THIS WORK."

and it's not just childhood, is it, because some days, she feels her head tied on only by a ribbon, and it's all she can do not to grab a pair of scissors. or maybe she's a paper doll, hand in delicate hand with mirrored self, and still her fingers twitch toward the scissors.

and there is this thing she doesn't have a name for, fingers scratching the skin of her thighs. she runs winter-fingers through her lover's hair, carries her grief like a burning plate of food. she quits her job and she quits another job, cutting through options like magazine pages that have stuck together. this spring, there are snails on every surface of her house. she steps on one in the kitchen, feels the crunch of it beneath her slipper, takes another from beneath her pillow and sets it outside.

when it's dark out and still hot enough to sweat, she sits alone beneath the lilac tree in the front yard. she calls it "holy," but that's not what it is.

october comes without a job. november comes without a job. freezing puddles soak through socks with holes where the butterflies tore through her closets last spring. another snail is in the bathtub. carry it to the windowsill. carry it through the neighborhood and knock on every door, praying for its owner to come claim it.

but no answer waits behind closed doors, only a gentle clicking sound, like scissors against silk.

Continue to page 48.

Situation #3

You are:

Calf deep in a pile of mildewed leaves, ignoring the itch of the ant bites on your ankles. The forever yard is in great disarray, and you feel wasp larvae underneath your ribs. All this time, you thought the sky answered to you. You counted stars in the night, watched their numbers dwindle and did not know why. You didn't notice the traffic men plant streetlights through your forest. How could you? You were a child. As an adult, you can now feel the tendrils of what will become rot against your skin.

And you:

a)   Lay your soft body into the leaves and close your eyes, listen to the stars and wait for sleep to overtake you.

b)   Tear through the rot, searching for whatever it is that's been lost there.

c)   Vivisect your body, digging larvae out from underneath your skin until you have enough to bury. Mark the grave, then leave for somewhere new.

If a, go to page 49.
If b, go to page 52.
If c, go to page 57.

a cure for sleepless nights

decomposition, n:
the state or process of rotting, decay.
"the decomposition of organic waste."

-from Oxford Languages, accessed online

when fatigue seeps into every vertebrae
and you sob at the touch of sunlight on your cheeks,
name it homesickness.

everything is process.

at least two-thirds of everything is rot.

so when the autumn wanders through the day,
follow it into a leafy bog.
let the hollows of your body be your guide.

listen to the itching of your skin
and lie down someplace where the earth is soft.

If the spell puts you to sleep somewhere uncanny,
go to page 50.
If you are left haunted by questions,
go to page 54.

lethargy

you awaken in the garden store, head
pressed against a tower of fresh soil
and ivy tendrils wandering your legs.

when the fractured winter sunlight hits your eyes
and you feel yourself half-dizzy, nearly blind,
don't call it greenhouse.

untangle your soft body from the weeds
and follow the path where bricks have torn through street,
and tree roots climb through bricks

until you make it to your own small bed.

*If you dream of a forest,
go to page 51.
If you dream of other lives you could have lived,
go to page 56.*

in the dream, there is

a city amidst the coniferous trees, filled with the fireflies
of midwestern childhood and that one summer in the alps,
your apartment building somewhere in the pines.

awake in the unlit city, branches pulled together so the rain has
a roof on which to pitter-patter,
fuzzy caterpillars making the skin of your arm itch
and neighbors somewhere in the distance.

you sit—

bark rough against your thighs beneath the lichen, leaving lines
against skin, moonlight pouring down the trees
and there are insects on the lilac trunk.

big fat ones, with hard shells, like you saw
at the apartment you like to think about on quiet nights,
how they'd climb the window screen

and this game of free association cracks you open.
there are so many lives, one inside the others, like those dolls
with a line down their middles, and when you open them

those spiny larvae drag their bodies out.

Go to page 64.

you do not have to hide it in your chest

everything you've ever lost sits in a box at the bottom of the ocean // in an egg inside a duck inside a rabbit // and you, the witch's favorite, wonder why you have not been eaten yet // did you remember the doll // did you remember to feed the fucking doll // you can't count on Prince Ivan this time // the same story keeps ending // keeps on fucking ending // and you still can't find your favorite cow skull necklace // still can't find your heart and the things you used to store inside of it // inside an egg // a duck // a rabbit // a box // buried deep beneath the soil // did you check in more mundane places // earrings lost in the washing machine and coming out in the dryer // did you find a new job // did you find a place to live // how fast can you keep moving through this quagmire?

Do you go looking, even under such circumstances?

If yes, go to page 53.
If no, go to page 60.

Vacancy

and when, after years of searching
for an answer, all   you come up with is
an empty box, how   long will you hold
onto it for? will you   hold it to your ear,
a cardboard seashell,   listen to the waves?
will it grow heavy in the   chiasmus of your arms?
will you grow attached,   will you cry the day you
have to set it down? will   it become waterlogged
and heavy, no clean   auspicious beast?
will the damp cause   it to shed its skin,
and will this bro   ken cardboard be
your bedding? will you forgive it?
will you forgive yourself?

a)   I need to start over with a different story.

b)   I need to better understand the box.

If a, go to page 56.
If b, go to page 55.

Why did you spend so long confusing the orderly lines of a
ribcage for your grave?
>Where has your connective tissue come unraveled,
>and what can it be woven into instead?
>>When the graveyard of ants was washed
>>down the bathtub drain, was that the final
>>time?
When did you last visit your elementary school?
>When did you last hold a snail in the palm of your
>hand, like you did each day for all of second grade?
>>Are you still half-soaked in childhood?
Which direction do the windows face in your apartment? Do
you long for sunset but see only wall? Are you lonesome?
>What exactly is the difference between "lonely" and
>"lonesome?"
>>How did this resin get beneath your
>>fingernails, and do you know the best way to
>>dig it out?

Will it be okay one day, even just for a moment?
>Will it make sense?
>>Will the birds line up across your rooftop to
>>sing to you, and will you have the time to
>>stop and listen?

Go to page 64.

On the Concept of a Box

What classifies as a box?

The light outside the window is gray and you have been home for far too many hours, building a storm drain in your bedroom walls. The cardboard pipes you laid have been soaked through.

What shapes can a box be?

A box is only so much empty space, empty where things used to be filled up. As a child, you had a red wool coat, bought for $1.25 out of a box at a garage sale, and you wore it when it went down to your toes and still when it went down only to your knees. Only solids retain their shape; everything else expands to fill its space.

Does a box have to have a lid?

If you want to save the rainwater for next summer's drought, a cardboard drainage system will not work. Dig a trench in your bedroom floor, beneath the spot where water flows through wall. Build a reservoir. Wear your favorite red coat in the bedroom so you don't grow cold through winter. It will not rain forever. It will not rain for even three more days.

What is a synonym for box?

You've seen pictures of yourself in that red coat, earmuffs tight around your ears and smiling, always smiling. You've seen pictures of yourself in the years since. Something new was given to you, an empty space you couldn't seem to fill. Everyone else is smiling, handing out dandelions and paper cards, and you, who did not get the message in time, hold only your breath

and a soggy cardboard lung.

If you build your home from cardboard,
go to page 63.
If you think about a home you lived in long ago,
go to page 61.

Timelines

in a kinder life, maybe you walk
down the tree-lined sidewalk,
supplying dandelions to people
on beautiful days

and you never mind turning thirty.
you buy a cabin in the North Cascades,
and it is quiet
and the forest never catches fire.

maybe the whole world shifts
when you're nineteen
and the crisis that split your life in half
doesn't take place this time around

and you sit on a summer porch,
daytime highs in the nineties, pen
light in your hand
as it flies across the page

and the final dregs of sunlight bleed through sky.

Go to page 64.

a different summer

and if you're missing me, you tell her, *you
should really do something besides imagine me.*
she says, *it is easier to love an imaginary girl.*
you ask her to water the tomatoes when
you're gone.

in the dream, you depart and return home to
tomatoes desiccated on the vine. the house is
empty. you imagine her there, but the sheets
are still unraveled from the last time you
made love.

and there is no moral to this story
because if there was, you would not
be able to bear it.

True or False?

If true, go to page 53.
If false, go to 58.

you call 911 but no one answers
so you ramble on a while until
the answering machine
cuts you off.

you call back and say,

*Please pick up. There's something in my chest
and I don't think it's supposed to be there.*

*If this is an emergency, go to page 59.
If not, go to page 60.*

Fourth Law of Motion

when it comes to bodies, no reaction may ever be
considered either equal or opposite.

59

Go to either page 54 or 63.

encroachment

sometimes, you tear out the ivy so it won't tear down the bamboo, and sometimes, when thinking about this, you do not consider that they're both invasive, and sometimes your fingers are so numb from touching ice that they cannot write well, which means they cannot write poorly, which means there will be no reason later to rip the pages out.

these days, you avoid crying at sad movies, even when the dog dies or someone realizes they can never return home.

you were left behind once, at home, like the kid in that Christmas movie, only there were no bandits or hair-brained schemes, and you didn't save the day, and no one hugged you for a very, very long time when they finally made it home. you were asleep in your bedroom. you were still asleep when they returned.

at the therapist's office, she asks you why, and you don't know the answer.

in a different life, you imagine yourself as a forest ranger. your cabin is safe from the elements and your bones don't ache, despite the physical labor. there is no internet and nobody can contact you. you don't miss your family because it's just a dream and dreams don't have to make sense. you tear out ivy with your bare hands, and it disintegrates between your fingers. there will be no forest fire this year, but the rivers go gray anyway, out of habit.

If you make yourself coffee, go to page 61.
If you visit the forest while it remains unburnt,
go to page 62.

November

Afternoon coffee, fingers
twitch against the cabinets
>>>>>>and it's gray outside the window.
the leaves were supposed to fully coat the ground by now,
>>>>slick sidewalks like when you were a kid
the way you slipped in the aisle of the bus and hit your head,
a memory that shouldn't send you anywhere soft inside your
mind
>>>but of course it does.

You are no longer a child.
You are no longer a child.
You are no longer a child.
>>>>>>But childhood still grips you
>>>>>>in its sharp canines
>>>>and stories you only now begin to understand.

Starting at the end helps.
Not starting at all is not an option.

>>>>>>>>You drink the coffee,
>>heart-inside-your-lungs-inside-your-ribcage.

The year you turned twenty-five, you lived in an apartment
>>>>with an electric fireplace
>>>but a furnace that barely emitted heat.
>>>Cocooned in blankets, coffee
>>>wrapped inside your hands.

There are many ways to survive the winter.

You used to think they were all the same
>>>>>but you don't think that anymore.

Go to page 64.

unspoken

The birds make all the noises in the forest   *for us?*
until you listen closer to the dirt   *(hurt)*
where beetles excavate the dying entrails   *gentle*
of trees that dug their tendrils in the earth.   *worth*

The trees that have been now reduced to cinders   *hinders*
the lichen growing underneath the bark.   *arc*
The rotten wood that creeps beneath your fingers   *lingers*
an echo that can't get the meaning right.   *bright*

There is a bruise inside your deepest being   *meaning?*
and in it wander beetles, moss, and worms.   *it burns*
The bridges rot from time, the pathway cleaving   *leaving*
you know now that you never can return.   *yearn*

Go to page 64.

The Empty Days

You imagine a roof over everyone's home except for yours. You want to ask them how they got the roof, and whether it protects them well enough. Your socks grow drenched against the carpet, and when there's lightning outside, all the windows in your house will shake.

And then some days, more jarringly, you will wake up with a pocket full of daisies that weren't there when you fell asleep. You'll wake up, and the smell of rain will be the smell of the forest that once lived here, a long time ago, with tiny trails of slugs on your front porch.

You wonder what inside of you created these gray skies, and what happened to your favorite blue umbrella. You beg for a weather forecast, but the numbers on the screen distort before your eyes.

In the mornings that taste of springtime, you won't know what to do with yourself. You will sit on your patio and watch fluffy clouds chase each other across the sky, and you will be angry, because it could have been like this every day and wasn't. You will be angry, because if it's worth it after all, then you don't get to give up.

You call your mother. She doesn't answer. You have a letter that she wrote you during what was once the hardest year of your life, tucked inside a cardboard box. You consider taking it out to read but don't.

"When?" you ask. "When will the daisies come to my pocket,
and when do I get to be angry at how
beautiful things are?"
We don't know.

The answer changes every single time.

Go to page 64.

Artifacts

[**Item 1:** *photograph of herself at three years old, wearing overalls and a hat with a sunflower pattern. she sits atop a giant rock and smiles.]*

[**Item 2:** *scrapbook page made by her parents at the age she is now.]*

> **Note on Item 2:** *she tries not to romanticize their life at the expense of her own, but still traces her fingers over the address of their first home.*

[**Item 3:** *newspaper article about a play written by her third-grade class, featuring a picture of her at age 9, head bent over notebook.]*

> **Note on Item 3:** *she remembers this as the year she began to have trouble sleeping.*

[**Item 4:** *flash drive containing digital images of her wedding, dress almost the color of sunflowers. she looks more like her mother than she will ever know what to do with.]*

[**Item 5:** *vision board for the past year, on which she included the words "feel," "unapologetic," "bloom," and "forgive yourself."]*

> **Note on Item 5:** *she'd cut out the word "grief," but left it off.*

Continue to page 65.

Situation #4

You are:

Just a girl, even after all this time; just a regular girl in a regular life with regular hunger pangs. There is nothing sacred about the ache between your fingers, just the strain of a pen gripped tightly for too long. This caesura occurs in every growing-up. It's happened to you before, but you've forgotten, as you will soon lose track of this one too.

And you:

Step out into your frigid living room one morning and see the shriveled orchids on the kitchen windowsill, but this time, you bring them gently from their pots. This time, you investigate the roots, see how they're brown instead of gray, how they couldn't possibly transmit water to the leaves.

You go to the store, pick up fertilizer and fresh orchid mix. You research humidity levels. It's been a difficult year, and after everything else, you can't bear to see withered, neglected stems.

You're careful as you exhume the roots, implanting them into their fresh new soil.

Continue to page 66.

Conditional Statements

If:

> you wake up one morning in a house with fresh rose
> petals on the windowsill
> and a single flower on the orchid's stem,

do not confuse safety for permanence.

And if:

> your stomach clenches at the dirt
> on your white carpet
> and the way you've only finally left your bed,

know this too:

it took months of ice cubes
soaking into soil
before roots slithered grayly from the pot.

So if:

> a single petal has uncurled

count up the days spent nurturing dead soil.

If you take the petals and put them in your tea,
go to page 67.
If you dust off the windowsill, go to page 68.

Beginning

Rose petals crushed into a jar of tea.
Believe that summer might just come this year.
The press of sunshine just won't let you be;
it wraps around your neck and whispers, "near."

You'll map the throughline of your crooked spine,
while fingers tiptoe lightly over skin.
This garden-morning, tepid summertime.
You fill the teacup, add ice to the brim.

Your body finds itself tugged toward the light.
You drink the tea, force petals down your throat.
Remember: it will not remain this bright,
no matter just how soft the white clouds float.

That sharp desire for sweetness rushes in.
Ant-like, you search for sugar in your skin.

If someone makes you breakfast, go to page 69.
If you are ready for summer, go to page 71.

A Prayer for Lonely Moments

Take a damp rag into your hands.
Undust the lavender from your attic baseboards,
and from the windowsill beneath your cactus

to grant the ants permission to return.

If you need a recipe, go to page 70.
If you go outside to watch the sunset, go to page 71.

Preparation

in the morning, someone makes you breakfast
crepe recipe from your father
homegrown tomatoes, cheese,
and basil from the garden

you find it difficult to talk about,
think, *love,* but somehow also think
if nobody loved me I'd be okay
I know how to make my own breakfast

and at the end of it all, has enough grown in your garden?
did you tear the rocks out of the soil with your bare hands,
dirt clogging the space underneath your nails,
did you water it enough,
did you remember to let the sunlight in?

and what will it take to stop the roll of questions,
trade it in for a life
in which you can notice the mushrooms growing
along the edges of the grass,
notice the crispness
of a tomato that you grew yourself?

For a different recipe, go to page 70.
To finish breakfast and sit on the porch,
go to page 72.

Ingredients

2 artichoke hearts, soaked in saltwater
Garlic grown in your own garden, left to rot and rejuvenate for
a three-year cycle
Fresh mozzarella from the farmer's market
          (holding hands as you duck under white canvas,
          protection from the rain)
Tomatoes, flour, and however much salt
you can summon while thinking about how much you've
changed from the girl that you were two years ago
1 packet of yeast

Use your hands to knead the dough, and pray.
You cannot watch it once it's in the oven.

If you need more signs of love in the world,
go to page 71.
If you need to watch the sunrise, go to page 72.

Retrospect

the sweat-stained orange sunset of July,
as your Birkenstocks pound against asphalt
and the heat still settles from the afternoon.

everything
          echoes

you can't be lonely tonight in any way that matters.

do not embroider the present with the past
do not center your weight on branches that might snap

but look back.

salt
is sharp and lovely on the tongue
and without it you are sluggish and confused.

when autumn comes, yellow light will
reflect from oil-stained puddles
and the sun will set at six in the afternoon.
you will remember being seventeen

and the weather channel predicting hail on the afternoon
of your first kiss

and you are no longer seventeen
and you have been kissed more times than you deserve
and *lonely* still envelops you at times

but not tonight.

Go to page 73.

Forgive

winter morning on the back porch, dark
giving way to light-gray streaks through clouds
and just like that, you've missed the sunrise

ice crystals biting the fraction of unhidden skin
between sleeves and hands
that grip cold coffee in a scalding mug

and just like that, hands tight against ceramic,
you make your decision

and despite the heat, you do not put it down

Go to page 73.

Permission

And in the end, was the body ever yours, or only borrowed? Speed up the tape to the end and watch as mushrooms start to sprout from skin. Wonder if you've read this story before, or only heard one like it, very long ago. Imagine yourself kind. Imagine others kind. Imagine a path through the forest that goes downhill the entire way.

And in the end, will it be over? Will whatever whisper of self that made itself known inside of you exist, even when all that remains is soil and the things that grow from soil?

Let's wind the tape back, a bit. You are here, and it is now, and that is all that you can ever be asked to carry. Just this body, in this time and place. It is a gift, although it may not always feel this way, and although the path cannot be just downhill. Like any gift, you must decide what to do with it.

Do you:

a)   Search for a place to set this body down?

b)   Bring it with you for a little longer, slipped inside the picture of yourself you carry from when you were very small, dirty pink dress and skinned knees but smiling, always smiling, so big that it barely fit across your face?

If a, return to the beginning.
If b, continue to page 74.

Epilogue

*what does it mean, a year later, when she sits in the bathtub
with her notepad once again, ink distorting as the pages soak
through? what does it mean to be in the same body, when
even the bathtub has since been replaced? water spills through
everything, in the end.*

*she eats dinner at a table covered in bills and grinds salt onto
every bite of food. she pours shots of peach liqueur and leaves
them for the fruit flies. she maps out her childhood on charts
full of characters who are all also her. she reads the footnotes
of her folklore books, fills the margins of any chapter that
pairs fairy tales with child psychology, even the Freudians,
peeling away the magazine pages she'd pasted over the text.*

*is there a story to all this, and in what order can she tell it? did
it ever begin or really end? in the year since she's chiseled
herself out of the ground, she's had to learn to be an epiphyte.
she waters her orchids, and watches the roots climb from the
pot, adhered to nothing.*

*on the bus, she hears a question that tangles in the space
beneath her skin. she draws Sisyphus in the margins of a love
letter*

his boulder centimeters from the top.

Acknowledgments

Gratitude goes out to the editors of the journals and anthologies who previously published the following pieces:

Jake Mag: "November"

Sad Girl Diaries: "Other Lines of Inquiry" (Previously "Six Questions to Ask Your Therapist Instead of Responding to Whatever it Was She Just Asked You")

About the Author

Hailey Spencer is, in the words of her wife, Elizabeth, "an absolute cloud of a girl." Her work runs in obsessive circles around fairy tales, grief, and healing. Her debut poetry collection, *Stories for When the Wolves Arrive*, was published through First Matter Press in 2022, followed by her chapbook *Out of Love in Spring* published through Finishing Line Press a month later. Since the summer of 2023, she has served as an editor and board member at First Matter Press. For more on Hailey and her work, visit her on Instagram @outofloveinspring or on her website haileyspencerwrites.com

About the Publisher

Escape the Mundane | Est. 2015

Follow us on:

Scan the QR code for www.thirtywestph.com